In The Eyes Of Mary

MA Guevarra Bono

Ukiyoto Publishing

All global publishing rights are held by

Ukiyoto Publishing

Published in 2022

Content Copyright © MA Guevarra Bono

ISBN 9789360163617

All rights reserved.
No part of this publication may be reproduced,
transmitted, or stored in a retrieval system, in any
form by any means, electronic, mechanical,
photocopying, recording or otherwise, without the
prior permission of the publisher.

The moral rights of the authors have been asserted.

This is a work of fiction. Names, characters,
businesses, places, events, locales, and incidents are
either the products of the author's imagination or
used in a fictitious manner. Any resemblance to
actual persons, living or dead, or actual events is
purely coincidental.

This book is sold subject to the condition that it shall
not by way of trade or otherwise, be lent, resold,
hired out or otherwise circulated, without the
publisher's prior consent, in any form of binding or
cover other than that in which it is published.

Dedication

To everyone who loved and hated me, who supported and doubted me, who embraced and pushed me,

> Thank you.

Contents

Ace	1
Agatha	2
Aliyah	3
Artemis	4
Aster	5
Barbara	6
Bechamel	7
Celine	8
Chantal	9
Cherry	10
Corazon	11
Corsette	12
Dorothy	13
Dulce	14
Ellen	15
Erin	16
Erza	17
Felicity	18
Frances	19
Gaia	20

Gretchen	21
Heather	22
Irene	23
Iris	24
Janine	25
Juliette	26
Krystal	27
Leona	28
Lilibeth	29
Lucresia	30
Luna	31
Mariam	32
Nabi	33
Nicola	34
Olive	35
Piper	36
Quiana	37
Reiju	38
Roma	39
Sofia	40
Stella	41
Sunny	42

Tabitha	43
Ulynn	44
Victoria	45
Wendy	46
Willow	47
Xanthe	48
Xiena	49
Yasmin	50
Zara	51
Darlene	52
Karen	53
About the Author	57

Ace

We ended,
not because we failed,
but because we surrendered.

Agatha

Love is either a blessing or a lesson,
I gasped, because you are both.
You were a blessing before you became a lesson.

Aliyah

Her eyes do not lie,
But her heart does.

Artemis

"I know what's the best for us!"
I watched the puppeteer break her own puppet.
Atlas! The *puppet* is free from her choking grasp.

Aster

Silence is her battle cry,
and that explains her victory.

Barbara

You stop feeding their ego,
And they will bark at you.

Bechamel

and the Sun
fell in Love
with the Beauty
of your Soul.

Celine

One day,
love will find you.
and it will stay.

Chantal

what is lovelier
than her face
is her soul
full of sincerity and love

Cherry

If I can do magic,
There will be more than one Earth,
And I will give you one,
in a silver platter.

Corazon

What hurts
more than a broken heart
cause by a cheating lover
is a broken friendship
cause by a *misunderstanding*.

Corsette

Even death cannot tear them apart,
What made you think that another woman will?

Dorothy

Promises
are something
we cherished,
and maybe
even after
it perished.

Dulce

'Distance is nothing', said the woman who promised him forever.

'Distance is everything', replied the man who can't gamble in love.

Ellen

his love is chaos

his touch is death

his kiss is a curse

and you're still sitting there

waiting for his embrace

Erin

he is immortal
a powerful being
undying, unyielding
not until he met his weakness
you.

Erza

If you did not let the snake deceived you,
you will never fall.
If you put a little more faith on me,
we could have it all.

Felicity

I love you,
You have to remember that.

Frances

"Leave!"
I shouted,
But my heart wanted you
to stay.

Gaia

The ocean and its waves,
The sun and its rays,
Perfect together,
cannot exist without the other.

Gretchen

She was never kind,
She was insolent.
She is difficult, and indifferent.
She is ugly, and a little bit crazy.
And you still embraced her,
with all your warmth and kindness.

Heather

Her life flashes bloodily before her eyes,

Like the murder scene she saw in a movie last month.

She trembled as she realized,

She is both the murderer and victim in her life.

Irene

She has everything yet has nothing to lose.
That makes her a dangerous woman.

Iris

Sometimes, it's you
Sometimes, it's me
But it will never be *us.*

Janine

She fell
In love
With his
Honesty

Juliette

'Please don't be in love with someone else', he whispered.
I sighed, knowing exactly you did.

Krystal

I yearn for you.
Every single day.

Leona

And that very same loneliness consumed her again,

Like a ferocious lion devouring its prey.

Lilibeth

She is one of a kind.
She said she would protect me,
> but I saw her putting poison on my tea.

Lucresia

She is both a fighter and a believer.
She has a beautiful soul.
But every beauty has a downfall.
When you look at her eyes,
you will see what I wish I did not see
There is sadness, and there is anger,
All hidden, and unspoken
The longing for freedom,
She wants to be free.

Luna

Your scars are not ugly,
The society is.

Mariam

I am standing,
In the middle of the battlefield,
Proud and unscathed,
Unwavering, covered in blood
but not mine.
I may look tough,
and rough at times.
But I am just a child,
I need your love.

Nabi

I know this is selfish,
But I hope I find happiness before you do.

Nicola

Sometimes,
We love too much,
And it kills us.

Olive

Bastard exes,

Present cheaters,

Stop *collecting* them.

You are a woman, not a trash can.

Piper

kiss the sun

feel the rain

close your eyes

and come back

COME BACK!

DO NOT LET THE BEASTS DETHRONE YOU!

RECLAIM THE CROWN!

Quiana

If he does not love you,
LEAVE.

Reiju

It was a vast ocean, and we drifted apart.

Roma

I know I can move forward as long as you are beside me,

How can the Earth survive without the Sun?

Sofia

The mention of your death still struck a nerve,
And I wish I was on your deathbed,
I wish I was there,
I wish I was with you.

Stella

Of all the love I received,
I always remember yours.
I may not be your favorite,
But I knew you loved me.
Not until *he* came,
I do not blame you.
But how could you forget me?

Sunny

I do not like the way I was blinded by your light,
And still yearning for your warmth.

Tabitha

She stabbed her,
And stabbed her again,
Until there's no more tears and blood pouring

Ulynn

You are a beautiful piece of poetry,
Free, and lovely
Everyone will try to read you
But not all will understand you.

Victoria

One day,
You will realize,
It's not meant to be,
Not because you are not enough,
But because you are too much.

Wendy

I let the sun burned my heart,
I let the sea drowned my soul,
I let the pain devour my whole being,
Because it makes me human,
It makes me feel something other than *anger.*

Willow

I heard it all.
The agonizing screams,
    The painful cries,
Everything echoed, and all I can do is listen
    To my old self
    To my broken past
And I am glad I woke up from that nightmare,
And now I know how to fight back.

Xanthe

She is war,
Not everyone can win.

Xiena

In that wretched town, ravaged by war
You found me,
>dying and hopeless.

Yes, you saved me from that hellhole
You gave me shelter, your home.
You made me your warrior,
>heartless, mindless.

The false paradise is too disgusting,
>I just wanna be another version of Judas,

Your Judas.

Yasmin

Loyalty
In a friendship
Is rare

Zara

She is pretty,

like the blooming flowers in their garden.

She is shining,

like the enthralling moon in the sky.

And there *he* is,

picking the right flowers and admiring the lone moon.

Choosing you.

Loving you.

And maybe you can love him too,

more than the love I could give him.

And that, I will be forever indebted to you.

Darlene

Someday,
you will understand me,
and accept me for *who* I am,
for *what* I am.
Not an evil villain,
      just a lost and lonely soul.

Karen

"Do not bite the hands that feed you, that's bad."
I let out a mirthless laughter,
then I almost cry.
Remembering the all too familiar hands,
rough, and calloused,
punishing, and controlling,
made me shiver with fear,
almost taking my breath away.
It will show the world that it feeds you,
       that it cares for you,
caress you with love and fondness,
as if it adores you.
But behind closed doors,
       the very same hands,

rough, and calloused,
punishing, and controlling,
it will strangle you,
into your nightmare,
to your death.

Ang Kulay Ng Pag-Ibig

May iba't-ibang kulay ang pag-ibig.

Madalas ay pula,

    tulad ng rosas sa hardin, katulad ng dugong nananalaytay sa ating mga ugat.

Ang kanila ay tulad ng sa araw, maliwanag at nag-aalab, *amarilyo*.

May iba't-ibang kulay ang pag-ibig.

Madalas ay pula,

    tulad ng rosas sa hardin, katulad ng dugong nananalaytay sa ating mga ugat.

Ang kanila ay tulad ng sa takipsilim, nag-aagaw ang liwanag at dilim, *kahel*.

May iba't-ibang kulay ang pag-ibig.

Madalas ay pula,

   tulad ng rosas sa hardin, katulad ng dugong nananalaytay sa ating mga ugat.

Ang kanila ay tulad ng sa bulaklak na aster, matingkad ngunit may halong lumbay, *lila.*

Balang araw ay nais ko ring umibig, hahanapin ko ang tamang timpla, ang tamang kulay,

   ako ay lalaya, mga ngiti ay sisilay, habang hawak ang tamang kamay,

sa araw na iyon, ako ay maghihintay.

About the Author

MA Guevarra Bono is an earthling who loves literature as much as she loves food. She started writing short stories during her high school years until her college days (the period of both self-doubt and self-love). She's also a fanfiction reader and she enjoys reading stories from different fandom--- anime, kpop, webtoon, random dramas, etc.

A Quezon Province native, MA is a private high school teacher in her hometown where she was able to share her passion in literature. She enjoys teaching subjects like Creative Writing and Philippine Literature. Apart from reading and writing, Mariel loves listening to different genres of music, and currently trying her best to learn cooking.

www.ingramcontent.com/pod-product-compliance
Lightning Source LLC
LaVergne TN
LVHW041221080526
838199LV00082B/1864